HOW MANY MILES TO
JACKSONVILLE?

TONY JOHNSTON

ILLUSTRATED BY BART FORBES

G. P. PUTNAM'S SONS · NEW YORK

For the people of Jacksonville, Texas, where
my father, David Leslie Taylor, was born and raised.

"A very ordinary little East Texas town,
but it's not ordinary when it's home."

Frances David Smyrl (My father's cousin)

—T.J.

To Mary Jo for her patience and encouragement.

—B.F.

Text copyright © 1996 by Tony Johnston. Illustrations copyright © 1996 by Bart Forbes
All rights reserved. This book, or parts thereof, may not be reproduced in any form
without permission in writing from the publisher. G. P. Putnam's Sons, a division of
The Putnam & Grosset Group, 200 Madison Avenue, New York, NY 10016. G. P. Putnam's Sons,
Reg. U.S. Pat. & Tm. Off. Published simultaneously in Canada. Printed in Hong Kong by
South China Printing Co. (1988) Ltd. Book designed by Gunta Alexander. Text set in Garth Graphic.
The artwork was executed in Windsor-Newton watercolors on cold press illustration board.
Library of Congress Cataloging-in-Publication Data
Johnston, Tony, 1942– How many miles to Jacksonville? / written by Tony Johnston; illustrated by Bart Forbes.
p. cm. Summary: The narrator describes the excitement of having the train pull into the town of
Jacksonville, Texas, when he was a boy. [1. Railroads—Trains—Fiction. 2. City and town life—Texas—Fiction.]
I. Forbes, Bart, ill. II. Title. PZ7.J6478Ho 1996 [E]—dc20 94-29348 CIP AC ISBN 0-399-22615-X
10 9 8 7 6 5 4 3 2 1 First Impression

Hull-gull.

Hands full.

How many?

Chant for a children's guessing game.
The object was to guess the number of chinquapin
nuts a person was holding in cupped hands.
The loser paid the difference in chinquapins.

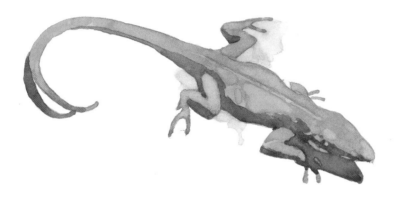

In Jacksonville, where I grew up, there wasn't much to do. We rolled tumbleweeds, played hull-gull with chinquapin nuts, and laid bets on the speed of lizards to pass the time. The train clacketing in was the most exciting thing that happened.

Mama said the kids started jumping like grasshoppers in a sack when the train came. The grownups did too.

Long before it pulled into the station you could hear the whistle blow. We all watched from the water tank, the highest point around. We closed our eyes tight and guessed where it was by the sound. We guessed how many miles to Jacksonville.

My sister, Lula, was a teenager. She didn't act like a grasshopper—more like a praying mantis, slow and quiet and creepy. She didn't want people to know she loved the train. So she watched from upstairs behind Mama's snowflake curtains. Quiet and creepy. We all hollered, "Train comin', Lula!" Those curtains swished down fast.

The whistle got louder and louder. Then, like a big old lightning bug, the train flew through the evening, steam rising through the pecan trees, and stopped near our house, spraying sparks and cinders in one long *hush*.

We swarmed from the water tank to meet the passengers, to say howdy and ask how things were in Louisiana and points east, from where the train had come.

The passengers came to eat at our restaurant, nick-named The Sour Rag. Before they arrived, the conductor telegraphed ahead how many would be there for supper. I hollered out the menu like a hawker at a ball game: "We got roast beef and roast turkey and roast potatoes and choice cuts of lamb. We got fancied carrots and collard greens and turnip greens and spinach greens."
If you favor greens, I added to myself.

The train was the T&NO, Texas and New Orleans. The HE&WT also passed through, though few people took it, the service was so bad. Papa called it the "Hell Either Way You Take It." Mama said, "That's the Houston East and West Texas. Now, hush up."

The engineer was my uncle, a train man from way back. He had a voice like a harmonica wheezing in and out. And he had train jokes to spare. His favorite was about the roundhouse, where trains go when not work-ing. "Run to the roundhouse, Rosie," he wheezed. "They can't corner you there."

My best friend was Pole Lovett, named for his fishing-pole legs. Days when a train stood emptied-out in the station, he and I boarded it. Sometimes Lula boarded too. We tasted leftover sugar-candy discs. We inhaled fumes from empty peppermint-candy sacks. We sat on the plush seats, polished bald by heads in places.

Down the aisles of the train signs were posted, such as, "Be nonchalant. Light a Murad."

Pole sneaked a Murad cigarette and lighted it. He was real nonchalant—till he started coughing. Then he like to choke to death.

Sometimes we went a ways down the tracks. I swear you could hear Lula's heart thump-thumping, though she moved like a mantis in prayer.

Some kids put Indian-head pennies on the tracks, which they picked up all flattened and ovaled-out after the train rolled by. I never did that. I couldn't spare a penny.

When the train came in, it dusted our town with cinders. It dusted Mama's snowflake curtains. And my sister too. Though she loved trains, she hated dirt. Being from a small town, we made our own soap. Lye soap. Lula's dream was to use only the soaps offered on the train. Like White King and Palmolive. Wrapper soap, she called it.

"Law," Lula told Mama when the train arrived, "I like to died from those filthy cinders. I could have soaped for a week."

She dabbed her eyes with a handkerchief and thought about the train. Though she'd never ridden it far, she said she longed to get fancied up and board the T&NO, to try every wrapper soap they had, all the way to Louisiana.

"How was the trip?" we asked the people when they stopped at The Sour Rag.

"Not half bad," they said. "Not half bad at all."

"Did you eat peanuts?" I was popping to know. "And sugar-candy discs? And peppermints? And jelly beans? Did you sip sarsaparilla? And orange Nehi? And cream soda?"

For a boy who played only with tumbleweeds, it was almost too much to know.

"We ate till we like to pop," said a biscuit-colored boy, all stuffed up with peanuts and Nehi.

"And were there toy monkeys climbing up strings?" I asked.

"Sure," he said. "Here's mine."

I wanted to spit in his eye for pure green jealousy. But Papa would have blistered me good.

"We used wrapper soap," said his mama. *"Palmolive,"* she drawled, so the word had near seventeen syllables.

"Law," breathed Lula, like a train exhaling steam.

The best thing about the train was the smell of
creosote, thick and heavy as blackstrap molasses.

No, the best thing was the cowcatcher with its sharp
metal teeth.

No, the best thing was mustard flowers crowding the
tracks with spring.

No, the best thing was the toy monkeys climbing
strings.

Sometimes it snowed in my hometown. Snow fell in a hush through the bare pecan trees—a lace curtain, whitening waiting trains. My dog rolled in it like a fool, snapping at the falling flakes. Snapping and gobbling and gulping snow the way he snapped up flies in summer.

Sometimes it hailed. We set tin pails out to catch it. Before it could melt, we sliced the hail with our Bowie knives and counted the layers inside. Then we popped it into our mouths like cold candy.

Sometimes it rained, but *rained*. Lightning zagged like blue wires across the sky. Our river rose. Sometimes a pecan tree fell down. Washouts carried the bridge trestles away, stranding train passengers. They might be marooned for a week.

My uncle gave them Murad cigarettes and Picayune tobacco to smoke—enough to stop a buffalo, its flavor was so strong. We tried to entertain them while they waited to be rescued. We played hull-gull and bet on the speed of lizards and rolled tumbleweeds.

When the relief train came, we waved at the departing passengers. They waved back.

"All aboooooooooard!" the conductor cried, stretching those words nigh on into the next county.

Then the T&NO rumbled off, gathering speed like a big old hardshell lightning bug flying farther and farther away.

I couldn't wait till the next train steamed in. Till I could greet the passengers and stroll up and down the aisle and sit on the plush seats and sample leftover sugar-candy discs and breathe peppermint fumes. Till I could close my eyes tight and hear the whistle getting louder and louder, and I could guess how many miles to Jacksonville.